The Path Of Bewilderment

M.Y. Hauger

Chapter 1

It was late in the night and Isabella Warrick was on her way home. It was a long day, and she couldn't wait to get back home, so she could relax.

As she was driving, she caught a glimpse of something on the road just ahead. As she got closer, he realized that it was a person that was lying face down on the road. She stepped on the brakes and then the vehicle came to a halt, and she put the vehicle in park. At first, Isabella was somewhat hesitant to get out of the car, even though it was obvious that the person needed help. Without hesitation, she took her cell phone and called for help. Then, she decided to get out of the car to see if the person was alright. She was nervous because she wasn't sure if he was dead or alive. She made her way over to him, and then she knelt down beside him before she carefully flipped him over onto his back. The front of his shirt was covered in blood. Isabella checked for a pulse and the man had one, but it was weak, and he wasn't breathing. She wasted no time as she cleaned the blood from his nose and mouth before she tried to revive him. Unfortunately, it seemed hopeless for the man because he wouldn't respond.

"Come on. Breathe." Isabella said.

She didn't want to give up. Isabella was determined to bring him back, even though it seemed like he kept slipping away with each minute that went by.

It was moments later when the ambulance arrived. The E.M.T.s made their way over to the man who remained unresponsive on the road. Chills ran down Isabella's spine and her heart sank because of how beak things seemed during that time. The E.M.T.s tore the man's shirt open and used defibrillator paddles to revive him, but he still wouldn't respond. Isabella gasped when she noticed how badly the man had been wounded and bruised.

"I'm sorry miss, his heart has stopped, he's lost a lot of blood, and he won't respond." one of the E.M.T.s said.

"Isn't there anything that can be done for him?" Isabella asked.

"I'm sorry, I'm afraid he's gone." the E.M.T. said.

Isabella's heart sank even deeper, and she felt even sicker after hearing that all hope for the man was lost. The E.M.T.s took the man, and then they left. Isabella was left speechless and sick to her stomach because of what had happened.

Everything happened so quickly that it hardly seemed real. Isabella watched as the ambulance drove away. Then she closed her eyes for a moment before she sighed. Suddenly, she felt as though someone had touched her hand. She was overtaken with chills as she glanced around. Isabella walked back to her car and got into it. She remained silent as she sat in the car and stared at the blood-stained spot where the man once was. As she sat there, she thought about how sad it was that the man's life had been cut so short.

Chapter 2

It was several minutes later when Isabella put the key into the ignition of her car, and then she started it. As she sat there, she continued to stare at the spot where the man was. She still couldn't wrap her head around what happened just a moment ago. As she sat there, she began to wonder if it was all just a horrible dream that happened so quickly that it almost seemed unreal. Then suddenly she became startled as her cell phone rang.

"Hello?" Isabella said.

It was her brother, Robert, who was on the phone.

"Hey, where are you? Is everything alright?" Robert asked.

"Oh, I was just on my way home."

"Okay. I just wanted you to know that I stopped over at your place, but I saw that you weren't home. I was worried, so I wanted to make sure everything was alright." Robert said.

"I don't know. I guess I'm fine. I think."

"You said you were on your way home?"

"Yeah."

"Okay then. I'll meet you at your place."

"Alright. I'll see you in a little bit." Isabella said.

She got off the phone, and then she sighed before she put her car in drive, and then she headed home. As she drove, she became depressed about what happened. She began to wonder whether the man had anyone in his life who would miss him. Isabella wondered whether he was married or if he was a father. Once again, she began to feel sick to her stomach, even as she continued to drive home. Isabella wished she could just forget about the man, but unfortunately, it was fresh in her mind, even as she continued on his way to her home.

Chapter 3

It was half an hour later when Isabella arrived at her home. Robert was already there, and he was waiting in the driveway in his car for her. After Isabella put her car in park and shut it off, she got out. Then Robert got out of his car shortly afterward. When he looked at Isabella, he could tell right away that something was wrong.

"Hey, are you alright?" Robert asked.

Isabella didn't respond.

"What happened?" Robert asked.

"Can we go inside and talk about it?"

"Sure." Robert said.

Isabella made her way to the door and unlocked it before she and Robert went inside.

"Okay, now that we're inside, talk to me. Tell me what happened." Robert said.

"I don't even know where to begin." Isabella said.

She walked over to the sofa and sat down. Then Robert made his way over to the sofa and sat down beside her.

"You could start from the beginning." Robert said.

At that moment, Isabella's eyes welled up with tears. Robert had an expression of concern on his face as he looked at his sister, who then spoke.

"It was awful. I was on my way home when I saw something on the road. As I got closer, I realized that it was a person, a man. He was lying face down on the road. I don't know for sure what happened to him. I think he may have gotten hit by a car or something. I approached him to see if he was alive. I turned him onto his back. The front of his shirt was covered in blood. He was unresponsive. It was terrible. There was blood on the road and blood was coming out of his nose and mouth." Isabella said.

"Was there anyone else there?" Robert asked.

"No. He was alone. If he had gotten hit by a car, whoever it was, wasn't there. They must have hit him and left."

"That's scummy. How could people be so careless?"

"I don't know. Anyway, I called for help. I even tried to revive him, but he wouldn't respond. When help arrived, they tried to revive him, but it was no use. They told me that he was gone and nothing could be done for him. They took him, and that was the end of it."

"I'm so sorry to hear that. It sounds traumatizing."

"It was terrible. I stood there for a moment, even as they left. I guess I was in shock. Everything happened so quickly that it almost seemed unreal. It was very strange because as I stood there, I swear, it felt like someone touched my hand. The thing is, no one else was there but me."

"That's creepy." Robert said.

"On my way home, all I could think about was him and how sad it was. What if he was married? What if he was a father who had children who were waiting for him to come home? It's sad to think that if it was the case, they'd be left waiting because he would never be able to come home to them. They'll never see him again. He was somebody's child at one time. What if his parents are still alive? How sad would it be for them to find out that their son's life was cut short."

"How old was he?" Robert asked.

"I don't know. He looked really young, possibly around our age or younger. He may have been old enough to have a family of his own."

"Oh." Robert said.

"I don't feel so well. I think I may turn in early."

"Will you be alright?"

"I don't know."

"I could stick around. Do you mind if I turn on the television?"

"No, I don't mind." Isabella said.

Robert grabbed the remote and turned on the television. The news was on, and it showed the man on the screen.

"That's him." Isabella said.

"It is?" Robert said.

"Yes."

"He does look kind of young, much too young to die."

"Right. I think I'm going to head to bed."

"Try to hang in there." Robert said.

Isabella walked through the hall to her bedroom, so she could try to get some rest.

Chapter 4

That night, Isabella tried to rest, but she was unable to. She tried to take her mind off of what happened, but she was unable to. The horrible moment played over and over in her mind. When she closed her eyes, she could see the man whose life was tragically cut short. Isabella sighed as she tossed and turned on the bed. Then she sat up before she glanced around the room. She put her hands on her head as she sat there quietly. Isabella sighed as she suddenly got a chill. She got off the bed and made her way to the window to see if it was open. When she approached it, she realized that it was closed. Isabella made her way back over to the bed, and then she sat down and covered up. She laid down and tried to get some sleep. Then she started hearing the sound of footsteps. Isabella also heard other sounds. She figured that it was probably just Robert. She didn't feel like getting up, even though she couldn't seem to fall asleep. Isabella had a terrible feeling that it would be a long night.

Chapter 5

The next day, Robert could see that Isabella was tired.

"Are you alright?" he asked.

"I couldn't sleep last night."

"Oh."

"I kept trying to take my mind off of what happened, but I couldn't. That horrible moment kept playing over in my mind."

"I really am sorry to hear that. I know this won't help much, but at least it wasn't someone we knew."

"Yeah, but unfortunately I can't unsee what happened. That moment haunts me like a bad dream. I wish it was nothing more than just a dream."

"I truly can't imagine what it must have been like to go through that experience. I have no doubt that it would be nightmare fuel."

"You have no idea."

"Listen, I'm here for you. In the meantime, I suggest you get some rest. I'd like to think that it would get better with time. Give yourself time to heal from it."

"Maybe you're right."

"You definitely need to try to get some rest. Being sleep-deprived isn't going to help you, in fact, if anything, it might make matters even worse. As for me, I think I'm going to go unless you need me to stay."

"I don't want to keep you from doing anything that you need to do. I could just call you if anything comes up."

"Alright then, try to get some rest. I'll give you a call, later on, to see how you're doing."

"I'd be happy if I could get some rest. I didn't sleep at all last night."

"Alright, then I should probably go. If you need anything, give me a call."

"Okay." Isabella said.

Robert left and Isabella went back to her room to try to get some rest. She sighed as she glanced around, and then she made her way to the bed and laid down. Isabella wasn't sure whether she would be able to get some rest. While she was up, she was exhausted, yet while she laid down, she found herself unable to rest. As she closed her eyes she once again saw the man who lost his life the night before. She wanted so badly to go to sleep, but she hated being continually haunted by that horrible experience. Isabella sighed as she closed her eyes and tried to relax on the bed. Then she opened her eyes as she suddenly heard something fall to the floor. Shortly afterward, she heard the sound of footsteps. Isabella began to wonder if Robert came back. She got up off the bed and left her room.

"Hello?" Isabella said.

She headed out to the living room.

"Robert? Is that you?" Isabella said.

As she entered the room, she noticed that there was nobody there. She checked the other rooms, but she saw no one. Isabella went back to her room because she wanted to get some rest. She made her way over to the bed and laid down. Then she closed her eyes as she tried to get some rest when suddenly, she heard the sound of a door closing. Isabella didn't feel like getting back up. She remained in her room as she hoped she would eventually be able to fall asleep.

Chapter 6

Later that day, Robert gave Isabella a call.

"Hello?" Isabella said.

"Hey, I was just calling to see how you were doing, just like I said I would. So, how are you feeling, anyway?"

"I'm still tired. I was able to fall asleep off and on, but I kept waking up."

"Oh."

"By the way, did you stop by earlier, like shortly after you left?"

"No, I went straight home." Robert said.

"Oh."

"Why do you ask?"

"It's nothing."

"It had to be something if you're asking if I came back even though I didn't."

"I was hearing sounds in my home."

"What kind of sounds?" Robert asked.

"It sounded like something fell to the floor. I also heard footsteps. The thing is, I went out to the living room to see if you were there, but there was nothing. Then I checked the other rooms, but again, there was nothing. I went back to try to get some rest, and then I heard a door closing.”

“Did you see anything?”

“I didn’t get up to see if there was anyone. I didn’t feel like getting up, and I figured that it would be a waste of time anyway.”

“You’re probably right. You know, it was probably your mind playing tricks on you. You know, I heard that a lack of sleep can cause a person to hallucinate.”

“But I wasn’t seeing things. I was hearing things.”

“Is it really that much different?” Robert asked.

Isabella didn’t respond.

“Do you know what I think? I think that you’re letting this whole thing get to you way more than it should. Of course,

it was sad, but you didn't know the guy."
Robert said.

Isabella said nothing as she looked at Robert and sighed.

"I know that it sounds easier said than done, but you need to try to move on from that. I realize that it's going to take time, but I feel like you're letting it bother you way more than it should. If you don't think you can get past it, get help. I realize that it's not something that you want to hear, but it would be better than letting it ruin your life." Robert said.

"I understand what you're saying. I hope that it doesn't come down to that. I'd like to think that it's just one of those things that I can eventually move on from. Maybe it's like you said, I just need time."

"Hopefully, but not too much time."

"Right."

"Well, I'm going to get off the phone. Maybe you could try to get more rest."

"Maybe."

"At least try. It's not good for you to not get enough rest."

"I know."

"Take care of yourself." Robert said.

"I'll try." Isabella said.

She got off the phone, and tried to get more rest.

Chapter 7

Several days had passed since the incident occurred. As time went on, it seemed to have gotten easier for Isabella and things slowly went back to normal. She was finally able to get some rest. Isabella rested for an entire day to make up for the times when she didn't get much rest.

After getting rested, Isabella decided to clean her home. Afterward, she went for a walk. It was a pleasant day with the bright sun and the warm breeze. Isabella was happy that things seemed to be going back to normal. She spent a good amount of time outside since it was a pleasant day.

Later in the day, Isabella and Robert went to a small café to get a bite to eat.

"It seems like you're doing better." Robert said.

"I am feeling somewhat better. I was even able to get some rest. I won't say that it never crosses my mind, but thankfully, it's not all I think about. Now and then, I do think about him and how sad it was for him and anyone he may have left behind."

"I know. It is kind of sad. What I'd like to know is what about the person who killed him? It seems to me like there should be some kind of investigation."

"Have you heard anything?" Isabella asked.

"No. There was nothing on the news, and nobody's saying anything more about it."

"There has to be something that's being done about it."

"You would think. The only thing that I can figure is that maybe they're keeping hush about it."

"But why?" Isabella asked.

"It's really hard to say. Let's just be thankful that we're able to move on. For a while, I was a little worried about you."

"You know, I think I'll be alright. At first, I wasn't sure, I mean, it was terrible, but it did seem to get easier with time."

"That's good." Robert said.

After they finished eating, they left the café and they both went home.

Isabella was thankful that she was able to enjoy the day.

Chapter 8

After Isabella got home, she freshened up for the evening. Then she grabbed the remote, sat down on the sofa, and then she turned on the television. She flipped through the channels until she found something to watch. As she sat there, she suddenly heard something falling onto the floor. Isabella got up and headed to the kitchen, where the sound came from. She glanced around, but she saw nothing, so she headed back to the living room and sat down. Then she heard another sound, so she turned off the television and went to her bedroom. She started to worry about whether there was a mouse in her house. Isabella sighed before she sat down on the bed. She sat there quietly for a moment, and then she laid down. At that point, she just wanted to get some rest. Isabella closed her eyes, and then she took a deep breath and released it as she tried to relax. Everything was quiet until, suddenly, she heard what sounded like a man sobbing. Chills went down Isabella's spine as she continued to hear the faint sobs. She hoped it would just stop. Isabella didn't feel like getting out of bed, even though the sobbing wouldn't stop.

Isabella reluctantly got off the bed and made her way to the living room. She thought that perhaps she forgot to turn the television off, even though she was almost certain that she had turned it off before she went to bed. As she entered the living room, she noticed that the television was off. She also noticed that the sobbing had stopped. Isabella went back to her room and laid down. For a moment, things were quiet until she heard a moan, and then the sobbing began again. Isabella pulled the blanket over her head because the sound was causing uneasiness, but at the same time, she didn't want to get back up. Isabella feared it would be a long night as the sobbing continued. She became discouraged because it seemed like the trouble had started again and just when she thought it was over.

Chapter 9

Unfortunately, the trouble didn't end that night. Isabella continued to hear things in her home. It was frustrating because every time she would search the premises, she would find nothing. Isabella wasn't sure if she should tell Robert about what was happening, especially since she could never find anything whenever she searched her home. As much as she hated the thought, she wanted to believe that it was possibly a mouse. The very idea of it was revolting to her, but unfortunately, she thought it would've been the best-case scenario for her. Then, there was the worst-case scenario which she feared was an even bigger possibility. The very fact that she kept hearing a man sobbing made her believe that the worst-case scenario was more than just a mere possibility. The very thought of it terrified her. She wasn't even sure if she even wanted to continue living there if that was indeed what was happening.

Chapter 10

As time went on, things started to go from bad to worse. Not only was Isabella hearing things in her home, but she was also seeing things, very disturbing things.

One day, as Isabella started to walk through the hall, she spotted what appeared to be blood on the floor. She didn't know where it came from because she knew for a fact that it did not come from her. Isabella sighed, and then she cleaned the blood off the floor, and then she washed her hands.

For a while, Isabella didn't think much about the spot of blood on the floor, but then she started seeing more and more of it. Sometimes it would be a spot or two, and other times there would be streaks of it, appearing as though something had been dragged across the floor. Isabella's stomach turned each time. She didn't understand what was happening and why there was blood on the floor, but she was perturbed by it. She wanted to tell Robert about it, but she was somewhat reluctant because she was afraid he wouldn't believe her, since nothing about it made sense. Each time Isabella searched her home, she found nothing other than the spots and streaks of blood that were left on the floor.

Chapter 11

Isabella wasn't sure about how much more she could take. It seemed like she was constantly cleaning up blood from the floor. She also continued to hear the sobbing off and on throughout the day.

One day, Isabella decided to go for a walk. She wanted to get out and get some fresh air and try to clear her mind. Without hesitation, she went outside and took a walk. It was a bit chillier than usual, but Isabella still wanted to get out of the house for a bit. As she walked, she thought about the things that were going on in her home.

She started to wonder about whether she should consider the idea of relocating.

After returning from her walk, she went into the kitchen to get something to drink. As she headed into the living room, she noticed something disturbing on the wall. Tension rose inside her as she looked at the words "help me" on the wall that was written in blood. Without hesitation, Isabella went into the kitchen and took a frying pan from the cupboard, and started searching her home, but she found nothing. Isabella sighed out of frustration, and then she took the frying pan back out to the kitchen, and then she got a bucket and filled it with hot soapy water, so she could clean the writing from the wall. Isabella's stomach turned as she looked at it, and then she cleaned it. After she was finished, Isabella took the bucket into the bathroom and dumped it before she cleaned the bucket out. Then she sighed before she washed her hands. She shook her head as she was becoming more and more disgusted with the situation that she was in. As Isabella looked into the mirror, she noticed something in the reflection that sent chills running down her spine. There, standing in the doorway of the room, was the man from the other night. He was looking right at her. The man was pale, and he had blood on his face. He trembled as he continued to look at her, and then he took a step toward her. Isabella screamed loudly, and then she turned around, but the man was gone. She nervously walked out of the room, and then she glanced around, but the man was nowhere in sight. Isabella's heart raced as she continued to look around, fearing that the man would jump out in front of her. She searched her home, but the man was nowhere to be found. Isabella couldn't take it anymore. She went to her room, packed some of her belongings, and then she got into her car and left. Isabella didn't look back as she drove away.

Chapter 12

Isabella was glad to get out of the house. As she drove further away, she sighed with relief. She hated that he had to leave her home in order to find peace. Isabella also realized that leaving would only be a temporary fix, and would never solve the actual problem. She hoped that, at the very least, it would buy her some time as she figured out what to do. Isabella was sure whether she would move or if there was something else that could be done. Her stomach turned as she thought about how the worst-case scenario was becoming a reality for her. She couldn't understand why it was happening. There was no connection between them, other than what took place during that horrible night. Isabella didn't feel that it was enough to cause the things that were happening in her home. It made no sense to her.

Isabella drove on until she came to a motel, where she decided to stop. She made up her mind to stay there until she figured out what to do. After she parked her car, she paid for a room and got the key to where she would be staying. When she went back to her car, she took her belongings from the passenger side of her car, and then she went to the door to the room, unlocked the door, and went inside. The room was nothing fancy, but she figured it would do until she figured out how to solve the problem she was facing.

Chapter 13

After she got her belongings put away, Isabella decided to relax and take it easy after having a stressful day. She thought for sure that she would be able to find peace since she was away from trouble. Isabella turned on the television, and then she sighed as she tried to relax.

As time went on, Isabella grew tired, so she decided to turn in early. She freshened up before she went to bed. Isabella closed her eyes as she rested on the bed. She sighed as she became more relaxed. Isabella was thankful for the chance to be able to have some peace without hearing disturbing sounds. There was no sound at all, just peace and quiet. Eventually, she started to drift off to sleep until suddenly, she heard the sound of footsteps. At first, Isabella didn't think much of it since she was staying at a motel, and she figured that it was possible to hear what was going on in the other rooms. Then she heard sobbing. As much as she wanted to believe that it was coming from another room, she wasn't sure if that was the case. She recognized the sound of the voice, and she knew that it was the same one that she heard in her home. At that moment, she began to wonder whether she would ever be able to escape the horrible nightmare that haunted her day by day and every night.

Chapter 14

The following day, Isabella decided that there was no point in staying at the motel any longer. With that, she packed her belongings and then headed back to her home. When she arrived, she got out of the car, took her belongings, and then she made her way inside. Isabella closed the door. She unlocked it, and then she made her way inside. Isabella closed the door, and then she glanced around. She hoped that she would at least get a brief moment of peace, since going to the motel solved absolutely nothing. Isabella took her belongings and put them where they needed to be. Afterward, she decided to go for a walk. After finishing her walk, she went back home and decided to relax as she watched something on television. Thankfully, there was nothing going on during that time. Although Isabella knew that it was wishful thinking, she still hoped that the trouble would be over.

Chapter 15

It was late in the night when Isabella woke up. As she opened her eyes, she became horrified because of what she saw. Chills overtook her as she realized that it was happening again. She wanted the trouble to be over, but it seemed like there was no end to it. Isabella panicked as she realized that she wasn't alone. There he was again. It was the man from the other night. Isabella's heart pounded in her chest as she looked at him as he laid there. Tension rose inside her as she wondered if what was happening was real or just a dream. Her hand shook as she reached out to touch him.

Suddenly, his eyes opened, and he looked right at her. Isabella's heart raced as she moved away from him and then fell off the bed. She got up and then she left the room. The man groaned as he got off the bed. Meanwhile, Isabella went to another room, and then, without hesitation, she went into the closet as she hoped that he wouldn't find her. She remained quiet as she stayed in her hiding spot. Isabella hoped that he would just go away, or it was just a horrible dream that was about to end. Suddenly, she heard the sound of the door as it opened. The man sobbed as he entered the room. Isabella's heart pounded in her chest as she tried to remain quiet as she hid in the closet. Then suddenly, the closet door came open. Isabella started to tremble as she realized that she had been found. She let out a scream, and then she tried to run, but then the man took hold of her hand. His hand was as cold as ice. He looked into her eyes as he whispered softly to her.

"Please, help me." he said.

Isabella was perplexed, and she wondered if it was indeed a dream that she was experiencing. It couldn't have been real. She was there when he was pronounced dead on the scene. As Isabella was about to touch the man's face, he fell down to the floor. Isabella helped him back up, and then she helped him to her room. When they approached the bed, she helped him onto it. Her heart sank as she looked at him. She could see that he was in pain. Then she looked at his side and abdomen where he had been bruised and wounded. Her heart raced, and her hand shook as she reached out and touched him. The man winced, and then he groaned as he laid on the bed.

"This has to be a dream." Isabella said.

"No." the man said.

As he looked at her, he took hold of her hand, and then he put it against the side of his face.

"You're freezing." Isabella said.

"Yes." the man said.

"So, this is really happening."

"Yes."

"But I saw what happened. They tried to bring you back. They pronounced you dead."

"Please, help me." the man said.

"Okay. I'm calling for help." Isabella said.

The man's grip on Isabella's hand became tighter.

"No." he said.

"What? But you need help."

"Please, don't."

"Why?"

"Because I want you to help me."

"But that's what I'm trying to do. You need medical attention."

"Please." the man said.

He had a sorrowful expression on his face as he looked at her. Isabella sighed and then she left the room. When she came back, she had several washcloths with her. She sat down on the bed, and then she started to wipe the blood from the man's face. He looked into her eyes as she wiped his face. She felt butterflies in her stomach as their eyes met. After she had finished cleaning his face, she took the other washcloths and started cleaning his wound. As she cleaned it, the man took hold of the blanket and squeezed it, and he winced as he lay on the bed.

"I'm so sorry. I really think that you should go to the hospital." Isabella said.

"No, I don't want to go to the hospital."

"But why?" Isabella asked.

The man didn't respond.

"Can you at least tell me what happened?" Isabella asked.

"I was hit by a car. Someone hit me while I was trying to cross the road. I suppose I wasn't paying attention. The thing is, they didn't even stop. They never bothered to see if I was alright." the man said.

"That's terrible." Isabella said.

After she cleaned the wound, she took the washcloths and left the room. Then she returned with some bandages.

"How are you not dead? They said that you lost a lot of blood and your heart stopped." Isabella said.

The man didn't respond.

"Why did you choose to come here? How did you find me?" Isabella asked.

"Because you did stop. I also know that you care. It made me realize that I had to find you and that if there was one person who would be willing to help me, it would be you." the man said.

Isabella finished bandaging him. She decided that it would be best to let him rest. She was about to get up and leave the room when he took hold of her hand.

"Please, stay with me." he said.

"But you need rest. I think it goes without saying that you've been through a lot, I mean, you almost died."

"Please, don't go."

"You need to rest."

"Please, stay here with me and let me rest against you." the man said.

"But we don't even know each other."

"Please." the man said.

"Alright, you win, only if it will help you to get some rest. I still feel like this has to be a dream. I know what I saw that night. It can't be possible that you're here." Isabella said.

She then sat down on the bed. Then the man looked at her before he moved closer to her before he rested against her.

"You're so cold." Isabella said.

She covered him up, and then she sighed as he rested against her. As he resisted, his eyes grew heavy until, eventually, he fell asleep. It wasn't long until Isabella also fell asleep.

Chapter 16

The next morning, when Isabella woke up, she suddenly remembered what happened the night before. She thought for sure that it was merely a dream until she glanced over and found the man next to her asleep. Isabella studied his face for a moment as he remained asleep on the bed. She still found it hard to believe that he was actually there with her, even though she was looking right at him. Isabella thought for a moment, and then she reached over and touched the side of his face. The man started to move. He moved closer to her until he was resting against her. Isabella covered him up, and then he sighed as he rested against her, and then he fell asleep.

Chapter 17

It was a half hour later when the man woke up.

"Is there anything I can get for you?" Isabella asked.

"If you mean something to eat, then no, thank you. I have no appetite."

"Are you sure?"

"Yes."

"Dare I ask when the last time was when you ate something?"

"I haven't eaten anything since that night."

"I still think that you should get checked out."

"No."

"But for all we know, there could've been internal damage done to you. You could die."

"No."

"I don't want you dying in my house. The other night was traumatizing enough. Not only that, I thought that you were haunting me, but now I have to wonder if you've been here the entire time." Isabella said.

The man said nothing as he looked at her.

"I can see that you're bound and determined to not go to the hospital, for some reason, even though I think you should. The very fact that you suffered a serious injury and have no appetite is concerning to me." Isabella said.

"Has it occurred to you that the injury may not be the only reason for me not having the desire to eat?" the man said.

Isabella sighed.

"Fine, then at the very least, can you at least try to drink something? At the very least, you should try to stay hydrated." she said.

"I suppose you're right, and I should try to drink something." the man said.

Isabella got him something to drink. When she gave it to him, he drank it slowly.

"I want you to know that I'm glad that you survived. It was depressing to think about how your life could've been cut so short. You look so young. Also, I couldn't help but think about the family that you may have left behind, had you died." Isabella said.

As the man looked into her eyes, his eyes welled up with tears.

"I'm sorry if I said something wrong." Isabella said.

A tear trickled down the man's face as he closed his eyes.

"I'm so sorry." Isabella said.

"No, don't be sorry. It's not your fault. It's mine."

"What happened?"

"I do not wish to talk about it right now." the man said.

"I understand." Isabella said.

The two of them said nothing more about it as the man rested. Before long, he grew tired until he went back to sleep.

Chapter 18

Later that day, there was a knock on the door. Isabella was going to get up, but then she realized that the man was asleep. There was another knock on the door. Isabella was going to try to get up, but she didn't want to wake the man up. Suddenly, she heard a sound. It was then that Isabella realized that it must have been Robert.

"Hello?" Robert said.

Isabella could hear that he was coming closer. Suddenly, there was a knock on the bedroom door.

“Is everything alright?” Robert asked.

“Yes. You can come in.” Isabella said.

Robert entered the door and entered the room.

“Why didn’t you answer the door when I knocked?” Robert asked.

Suddenly, he seemed perturbed when he noticed the man asleep on the bed.

“What’s going on here?” Robert asked.

“It’s not what you think.”

“Then what is it?”

“It’s him.”

“What do you mean?”

"It's the man from the other night."

"You're joking, right?" Robert said.

Isabella didn't respond.

Robert glanced at the man before he walked over to the bed to get a closer look at him.

"That's impossible." he said.

"That's what I thought."

"It said on the news that he was pronounced dead. You told me that he lost a lot of blood. How is he alive? How and why is he here?"

"Apparently he wanted to find me."

"This doesn't make any sense."

"I know, but I'm so relieved that he didn't die." Isabella said.

She looked at the man as he slept, and then she smiled.

"To be honest, I actually think he's kind of cute." she said.

"Are you crushing on him?"

"I don't know. Maybe, I mean, look at him. He's adorable."

"But how much do you really know about this guy? For all we know, he could be a fugitive that was fleeing from the law."

"I don't think so."

"You never know."

"I really don't think that he's a criminal."

"Just because he's attractive doesn't mean that he's good. Not all bad guys are ugly."

"He's not a bad guy."

"Okay, okay, I get it. It's obvious that you're into him. Just, please, be careful. I don't want to ever find out that he hurt you."

"Robert, he's in no condition to hurt anyone. To be honest, I think he's hurting, and I don't just mean physically."

"Why?"

"I don't know. He wouldn't tell me. He told me that he didn't wish to talk about it."

Robert then looked at the man.

"You know, I just realized something about him." he said.

"What?"

"He kind of reminds me of that guy that you had a crush on years ago."

"What guy?" Isabella asked.

"You know, that tall one with dark hair and unusual eyes. The one who owned that diner that burnt down, who always dressed in orange."

"Oh, that guy."

"Yeah."

"That was one beautiful man. He was so tall and handsome. He had the most beautiful eyes and those long dark eyelashes. He also had an amazing voice. He always smelled so nice. I also heard that he was a good kisser."

"I wouldn't know." Robert said.

"Neither would I, unfortunately. It was too bad he wasn't younger. I heard that he always looked younger than his age, but I still knew that he was older than I was. I had a crush on him for a long time, in fact, he was my first and only crush. I even dreamt about him."

"I think the entire neighborhood knew that you had a crush on him."

"Do you think he knew?"

"I don't know."

"I often wondered about what happened to him. No one ever heard from him or saw him after the diner burnt down."

"Some believe that he died there."

"I hope not. That would be horrible if he did." Isabella said.

"Like I said, I noticed that this guy looks a lot like him, except he has lighter hair and a lighter complexion." Robert said.

Then Isabella looked at the man's face, even as he slept.

"You're right. He doesn't have dark eyelashes, hair, or complexion, but he really does look like him. He's even tall like him."

"Does he have that unusual eye color like him?"

"No. I think his eyes are gray."

"Is that the reason you're into him?" Robert asked.

"To be honest, it didn't occur to me until you pointed it out." Isabella said.

Robert sighed.

"Like I said, just be careful. If you need anything, give me a call." he said.

Then he left his sister's home.

Chapter 19

Everything became quiet after Robert left. Isabella thought about the conversation she had with him, especially when they talked about her first crush and how the man who was in her home looked like him. Then she looked at the man as he remained asleep. She continued to think about the conversation she had with Robert and as she kept her eyes on the man, she suddenly felt butterflies in her stomach. Isabella became tense as she closed her eyes. She was about to kiss the man when he woke up.

"What are you doing?" the man asked.

Isabella said nothing as she looked at him nervously.

"I asked you a question." the man said.

Isabella still didn't answer. The man looked at her as though he was waiting for an answer from her.

"Is there a reason you can't answer me?" the man asked.

"I was just curious about something." Isabella said.

"What were you curious about?" the man asked.

"It…it was nothing."

"Right." the man said.

Isabella looked into the man's eyes as he kept them on her. She studied his face for a moment before she turned and was about to leave the room. The man took hold of her hand, and Isabella turned and looked at him.

"Do you need something?" Isabella asked.

"May I have something to drink?" the man asked.

"Sure. Would you like something to eat?"

"No, thank you. I'm not hungry, however, I could use some company. If you could, I would like for you to sit with me."

"Alright." Isabella said.

She then got him something to drink. She sat down beside him just as he requested. The man thanked her before he took a drink.

"I want to thank you for taking care of me. You have no idea how much

I appreciate it. If only there was a way to show you how much I appreciate it. Perhaps I could even satisfy a certain curiosity of yours." the man said.

Isabella became tense as she and the man looked at one another. The man then closed his eyes as he was about to kiss her. Then he stopped himself. He opened his eyes and he looked at her with a sorrowful expression on his face.

"No, I'm sorry. I can't." he said.

"Oh."

"I'm truly sorry."

"I understand. We don't know each other, and it's too soon."

"Right. I really don't know what I was thinking. I apologize. I didn't mean to be a tease." the man said.

He still had a sad expression on his face as he looked into Isabella's eyes. Suddenly, she was reminded of the time when she saw her first crush when he was sad, and her heart sank even deeper.

"Please, don't be upset. I said that I understand." Isabella said.

The man said nothing as he kept his eyes on her.

"You are so…" Isabella said.

She stopped herself before she finished what she was about to tell him.

"What?" the man said.

"No, it's nothing. Never mind."

"Oh." the man said.

Isabella could see that he knew that it wasn't just nothing.

"Maybe I should just let you rest." Isabella said.

“Perhaps.”

“If you'd like, I could stay here with you.” Isabella said.

The man just looked at her for a moment. He hesitated for a moment before he moved closer to Isabella before he rested against her. He looked into her eyes, and then she felt butterflies in her stomach again. Isabella hugged him tightly as he rested against her. Everything became quiet at that moment and eventually, the man fell asleep.

Chapter 20

Isabella continued to take care of the man. She tried to make him as comfortable as possible while he was there. Isabella also kept his wound cleaned and bandaged. She didn't mind taking care of him, since she found him attractive. Isabella often felt butterflies in her stomach as she took care of him, especially when they looked into each other's eyes. As time went on, Isabella found herself becoming more and more attached to the man. She tried not to show it, since it was getting harder to keep it to herself with the time he was there with her.

For a while, the man didn't want to eat. He kept saying that he had no appetite. Isabella continued to worry about him, even though his health didn't seem to be declining. Even though he didn't want to eat, Isabella still made sure he was hydrated.

The man spent a great deal of time resting. Some of the time he wanted Isabella to stay in the room with him. She did as he wished because she didn't want him to be put under stress. He'd often rest against her and now and then, he would take hold of her hand, causing Isabella to feel butterflies in her stomach. There were times when it seemed as though something would happen between the two of them yet nothing ever happened. Most of the time, he would stop himself before something would occur. Then he would just look at her with sad eyes. As much as Isabella wanted it to happen, she could see that the man was reluctant. She didn't want to push him into doing anything that he didn't feel comfortable doing. As much as she would've liked to be in a relationship with him, she didn't want to force it to happen. The last thing she wanted to do was stress him out when he was still in the healing process.

Isabella still found it hard to believe that he was there in her home. Now and then, she still wondered if it was a dream that she would soon wake up from. If it was, she hoped that it would never end.

Chapter 21

As time went on, Isabella noticed that the man seemed to be depressed. A part of her wanted to ask him if something was wrong, but then she thought back to several days before when he was almost in tears. During that time, he didn't seem to want to talk about whatever it was that was bothering him. With that in mind, Isabella decided that it was probably best if she didn't say anything at all. She also figured that if he wanted to talk about it, he would open up to her on his own.

Isabella felt sad for the man because it seemed like he continued to become more and more depressed as time went on. Now and then she would find him trying to fight back tears. Other times, when she entered the room, she found him with his hands cupped to his face as he wept bitterly. Many times, he tried to hide it, but it got harder for him with time.

Even though the man didn't open up to Isabella about what was bothering him, he still wanted her to comfort him. Even though she didn't really know what to do to make him feel better, she tried to do all she could to ease his pain. Most of the time, he just wanted to stay close to him. Oftentimes, he would rest against her. Sometimes, when he seemed depressed, Isabella would give him a hug. She wanted him to know that whatever it was that was upsetting him, he didn't have to go through it alone.

Chapter 22

Isabella continued to take care of the man and give him comfort. She felt sad for him because she could see that he was still depressed.

"I wish I knew what I could do to help you, but since I don't exactly know what's wrong, I feel like my hands are tied." Isabella said.

The man said nothing as he looked at her.

"On a more positive note, your bruises don't look as bad and the wound seems to be healing, in fact, it seems to be healing a lot quicker than I thought it would." Isabella said.

The man remained silent as he looked at her with a sorrowful expression on his face.

"Are you still in a lot of pain? I said before that you should've gotten checked out. You know, it's still not too late to do that." Isabella said.

"No."

"Don't get upset. I just want to make sure that you're doing alright." Isabella said.

The man didn't respond.

"By the way, I don't think we ever had the chance to properly introduce ourselves to one another. It's kind of silly, really. After all this time, we still don't even know each other's names." Isabella said.

The man said nothing.

"Okay, it seems like you just want to be left alone. In that case, I'll leave the room and let you rest." Isabella said.

She was about to leave the room when the man spoke.

"The name's Jayden Williams." he said.

Isabella turned and looked at him.

"You wanted to know my name, did you not? My name is Jayden Williams." he said.

"My name is Isabella Warrick."

"Please, stay here with me."

"I figured that you wanted to be left alone." Isabella said.

"No, I don't. I'd rather you stay here with me. I need to be comforted."

"Can you tell me what's wrong?" Isabella asked.

Jayden didn't respond.

"Alright, I'll stay here with you." she said.

"Thank you." Jayden said.

Isabella then sat down beside him. Then Jayden looked at her for a moment before he moved closer to her, and then he rested against her.

"I really do wish that there was something that I can do for you, but since I really don't know what's wrong, I'm not sure how to help you." Isabella said.

"But you've been helping me. You've been taking care of me and I truly appreciate it."

"Yes, I know, but what I'm talking about is your emotional pain. Something obviously has you upset."

"Yes, but as I said, I don't wish to speak about it." Jayden said.

"I understand, and I won't push you into talking about it, even though I worry about you. I will say that if you do ever want to talk about it, don't be afraid to. I want to help you." Isabella said.

Jayden looked into Isabella's eyes for a moment, and then he sighed as he rested his head against her before he spoke.

"Thank you. I truly appreciate everything that you're doing for me. I knew that I came to the right person for help, wherever I came to you." Jayden said.

Isabella was about to tell him how she felt about him, but then she stopped herself. She wasn't sure whether the time was right, or if it was best just to keep her feelings to herself.

Chapter 23

For a while, Jayden refused to talk about what it was that was bothering him. Then one day, he decided to open up to her.

"You were wanting to know what it was that's been bothering me." he said.

"Yes. Why are you so depressed all the time?" Isabella asked.

"The truth is, I have a broken heart. You see, I'm a married man and I do have a family, but unfortunately, things went wrong. I made a mistake. I did something that I shouldn't have done. Because of what I've done, I fear that my wife may not love me anymore. I'm afraid that she no longer wants anything to do with me." Jayden said.

"Oh."

"You must understand that I am weak whenever it comes to certain things, but at the same time, I want to remain true to her, even if she wants nothing to do with me." Jayden said.

Tears filled his eyes as he looked into Isabella's eyes.

"I'm so sorry." Isabella said.

"What am I supposed to do? I want to go back to her, but I'm not even sure if I know where she is. She may have gone away. I'm usually good at finding people, but unfortunately, things are different now when it comes to her. Furthermore, I'm afraid to face her after what I did. I know that I upset her. It was never my intention. I just did what I felt I needed to do. I regretted what I did afterward, and I knew that she was upset. It was for that reason that I panicked, and then I fled."

"I'm really sorry."

"I ruined everything, all in one day. I tried so hard to keep everything together, only to have it explode in my face in the end." Jayden said.

At that moment, he broke down and wept. Isabella felt sad for him, and he sat down beside him and hugged him as he wept bitterly. Isabella tried to comfort him. She hugged him even tighter as she spoke to him.

"I wish I knew what to do to help you, but unfortunately, I don't. The only thing I can do is be here and try to comfort you. I can show you that you're not alone." she said.

"I understand that, and I can't stress enough how much I appreciate what you do for me, but I have to find her.”

“I understand, but for now, you need to stay here. You’re still healing. You almost died. I don’t want anything to happen to you.”

“But you said that I was healing.”

“Yes, I know, but you’re not fully healed. If you go out now, something might happen now. You’re in no condition to go out there now. I don’t want anything to happen to you.” Isabella said.

Jayden looked at her, and then he sighed before he spoke.

“Perhaps you’re right, but at some point, I’m going to want to search for my family. I miss them and I want to go back to them where I belong.”

Chapter 24

As time went on, Isabella's crush on Jayden grew into something more. At first, she tried to hide it because she knew that he missed his family and he was upset because he felt that he couldn't be with them. What she didn't realize was that he picked up on her feelings toward him rather quickly. As time went on, and as her feelings toward him grew stronger, he started to ask her to stay in the room with him less and less. Of course, it didn't stop her from wanting to be in the room with him.

Most of the time, Jayden was quiet, and when Isabella tried to make conversation with him, he usually just gave her short responses. One day, she decided to confront him about it.

"Are you okay?" she asked.

"Why do you ask?"

"Because you don't seem very talkative."

"I suppose there's not much to talk about."

"I think there could be plenty to talk about."

"Such as?"

"Where are you from? Are you from around here?" Isabella asked.

"Yes, as a matter of fact, I am. Why do you want to know?"

"I was just wondering."

"Right."

"Have you always lived in this area?" Isabella asked.

"Yes, in fact, I grew up in this area."

"Interesting."

"How so?" Jayden asked.

"I can't help but notice the fact that you remind me of someone who used to live in this area." Isabella said.

Jayden frowned.

"Is that right?" he said.

"Yes. I often wondered about what happened to him. No one has seen or heard from him in years. You look a lot like him, except you have a lighter complexion and hair color. Also, your eyes are a different color from his."

"Let me guess, he had purple eyes."

"Yeah, as a matter of fact, he did. Do you know him? I mean, there has to be some sort of connection between you and him because you look like him." Isabella said.

Jayden became irritated.

"I can see where this is going, and you can stop right there." he said.

"Why? Did I say something wrong?"

"I'm so sick and tired of people comparing me to the king. He and I are nothing alike."

"I wasn't talking about the king. I never saw him, although I heard that he's a very beautiful man." Isabella said.

Jayden scoffed.

"Of course." he said.

"Look, I'm sorry if I upset you."

"Right, if you weren't talking about him, then who were you talking about? I'm not sure whether you're aware of it, but that particular eye color is very rare. There are only three people that I know of who have that eye color, and he is one of them."

"I never saw the king. As for the person you remind me of, it doesn't matter because he's not around anymore. Some people think that he died."

"I see." Jayden said.

"Look, I didn't mean to upset you. I was just trying to make conversation with you. I was also trying to make a connection since you look like someone who used to live in the area." Isabella said.

Jayden didn't respond.

"Maybe I should just let you rest." Isabella said.

She then left the room since Jayden seemed to want to be left alone.

Chapter 25

Later that day, Isabella went into the room to check on Jayden. She said nothing to him since it seemed like it did no good to say anything anyway. When she saw that he was alright, she turned and was about to leave the room when Jayden spoke.

"Stop." he said.

Isabella turned and glanced at him.

"I want to apologize for earlier." Jayden said.

"You're forgiven." Isabella said.

She turned and was about to walk away.

"Please, don't leave." Jayden said.

"Do you need something?" Isabella asked.

"Please, sit down with me." Jayden said.

Isabella hesitated for a moment before she made her way over to him and sat down.

"I feel terrible about how I acted, and I was wondering if there was a way to make it up to you." Jayden said.

"That's not necessary." Isabella said.

"You know, I overheard you talking about me to your brother. Correct me if I'm wrong, but I do believe that you told him that you thought I was cute." Jayden said.

Isabella suddenly became nervous as she looked into his eyes.

"Stay calm. There's no need to be nervous." Jayden said.

Then he moved closer to her.

"Have you ever been in a relationship before?" Jayden asked.

"N… No."

"Is that so?"

"Yes."

"I sense that you're a little nervous. Perhaps I could help to ease your tension." Jayden said.

Isabella's heart pounded in her chest as Jayden kept his eyes on hers as he gently touched the side of her face. Then he closed his eyes as he gave her a kiss. Isabella closed her eyes as they continued to kiss. Then Jayden looked into her eyes as he spoke.

"How about you move closer?" he said.

Isabella moved closer.

"Closer." he said.

She moved closer.

"Come closer." Jayden said.

Isabella kept moving closer. Jayden smiled as he looked into her eyes. Then they closed their eyes as they were about to kiss. Then Isabella opened her eyes.

"But I thought…" Isabella said.

"Shhh." Jayden said.

Then he gave her another kiss.

"I'm confused." Isabella said.

"Why are you confused?" Jayden asked.

"Because not long ago, you were depressed because you were afraid your wife won't love you anymore because of something you did. I won't ask about it, however, I would like to know why you're behaving differently." Isabella said.

Jayden didn't respond.

"Are you alright?" Isabella asked.

"No, I'm not." Jayden said.

Then he sighed.

"I didn't think you would oppose, after all, do you not have feelings for me? Also, were you not curious about something?" he said.

Isabella didn't respond.

"I'm sorry. It's just that I'm feeling lonely right now, and I was hoping that you could help me out." Jayden said.

Isabella sighed as she looked at Jayden, who looked at her with sad eyes. Then he touched the side of her face as he gazed into her eyes. They closed their eyes as they kissed. He smiled as he looked at her, and then he spoke.

"Thank you for understanding, and I hope that I've satisfied your curiosity." he said.

"Yes, I can honestly say that you have."

"Are you disappointed?"

"Not in the least."

"Is there anything else that you're curious about?" Jayden asked.

Isabella didn't answer as they looked into each other's eyes. Then

Jayden kissed her before he hugged her tightly, letting her know that he wanted her to stay with him for a while.

Chapter 26

The next day, Jayden seemed even unhappier than usual.

"What's wrong? Are you feeling alright?" Isabella asked.

"No, actually, I'm not."

"What's the matter?"

"I made a mistake. I let something happen that shouldn't have happened."

"Are you talking about what happened yesterday?"

"Yes, as a matter of fact, I am. You see, I'm a married man. It shouldn't have even been a thought."

"I'm sorry."

"Perhaps I should go."

"No, please don't."

"Why not? Nothing good could ever come out of this situation. I should've never come here in the first place."

"But had you not come here, you may have died." Isabella said.

Jayden said nothing as he looked into her eyes.

"I don't think you should leave." Isabella said.

"Why not?"

"Because you're in no condition to leave."

"But can't you see that this is wrong?"

"No, because I care about you. You're still not fully healed. Also, I can see that you're still hurting. You shouldn't be alone."

“But it's not good for me to be here. The truth is, I have a confession to make.”

“What is it?” Isabella asked.

“I have feelings for you, and I'm not sure how I feel about it. As I told you before, I belong to another, and I love her very much, but the thing is, during the time we spent together, I've grown quite fond of you.”

“What are you trying to say?”

“I'm saying that I'm sorry. I never meant for it to happen.”

“But you told me that she may not want anything to do with you anymore.”

“It doesn't change how I feel. I still love her. It also doesn't change the fact that I'm married to her, regardless of whether she does or doesn't want anything to do with me.”

"What if she doesn't love you?" Isabella asked.

Jayden said nothing as he looked at her with a sorrowful expression on his face.

"I know that you may not want to hear this now, but maybe someday, you could start over. We've grown very close to one another, and it was only in a short amount of time. Maybe she was never the one to begin with." Isabella said.

"That's not how I see it."

"I'm in love with you." Isabella said.

Jayden said nothing as he looked at her.

"Please, give us a chance. I truly believe we could be happy together." Isabella said.

Then she kissed him before she continued to speak.

"At the very least, let me be here for you, at least until you find her. You'll never have to be alone. If you do find her, and she wants to be with you, I'll understand. If she doesn't, I'll still be here for you." Isabella said.

Jayden sighed and then he spoke.

"Very well, but only because you somehow convinced me to stay. Also, I don't want to be alone, and I do happen to enjoy your company, even though I haven't always shown it. For that, I apologize." Jayden said.

"You don't need to apologize. I understand. At least you don't ever have to be alone. Even if you don't find her, or you do find her, and she no longer wants anything to do with you, you will still have me. I'll always be here for you, I promise."